KU-754-200

Buster and the Golden Glove

Kaye Umansky
illustrated by Leo Broadley

SCHOLASTIC

DUDLEY PUBLIC LIBRARIES

L 46682

653941   SCH

JJ

Scholastic Children's Books,
Commonwealth House, 1-19 New Oxford Street,
London, WC1A 1NU, UK
a division of Scholastic Ltd
London ~ New York ~ Toronto ~ Sydney ~ Auckland
Mexico City ~ New Delhi ~ Hong Kong

First published by Scholastic Ltd, 2003

Text copyright © Kaye Umansky, 2003
Illustrations copyright © Leo Broadley, 2003

ISBN 0 439 97858 0

All rights reserved

Printed and bound by Tien Wah Press Pte. Ltd, Singapore

10 9 8 7 6 5 4 3 2 1

The rights of Kaye Umansky and Leo Broadley to be identified as the author
and illustrator of this work respectively have been asserted by them in accordance
with the Copyright, Designs and Patents Act, 1988.

This book is sold subject to the condition that it shall not, by way of trade or
otherwise, be lent, resold, hired out, or otherwise circulated without the
publisher's prior consent in any form of binding or cover other than that in
which it is published and without a similar condition, including this condition,
being imposed upon the subsequent purchaser.

Buster and the Golden Glove

Schools Library and Information Services

S00000653941

Buster Gutt

Join Buster and his gruesome crew
for more piratical adventures!

 Be sure to read:

The Big Mix-up

Buster's Big Surprise

... and lots, lots more!

Chapter One

Buster Gutt, the pirate chief, had something on his mind. His ship, *The Bad Joke,* was heading for port after long weeks at sea – but Buster didn't seem a bit excited about it. He stayed all day long in his cabin, muttering to himself. He was even off his favourite food, sea pie!

The crew went along to find out what was wrong.

"What's up, Captain?" asked Timothy Tiddlefish, the cabin boy, who always had a cold. "We're worried ab – *achooo!*"

Buster gave Timothy a dark look.

"Goldglove," he growled. "*He's* what's up."

"Oh," sighed Timothy Tiddlefish. "Right. Him again."

Privately, he felt that Buster was becoming a bit obsessed.

Admiral Ainsley Goldglove was Buster's arch-enemy. He sailed around in the *HMS Glorious,* rounding up pirates and bringing them to justice. He was always in the papers. His trademark was a golden glove, which he wore on his left hand. People queued up to touch it for luck!

"Dunno why you're so upset, Captain," said Threefingers Jake, the bosun. "Ain't caught us yet, has he?"

"Right," agreed Crasher Jackson, the helmsman. "He tries, but we always escapes."

"Only by the skin of our teeth," argued Buster. "An' we never comes out of it well."

This was true. Buster and the crew had had several unfortunate run-ins with the admiral.

"Forget him, Captain," advised Jimmy Maggot, the cook. "Eat some pie. I done it with extra tentacles, the way you likes it."

"Ain't healthy, all this broodin'," agreed One-Eyed Ed, the lookout.

"I agree," said Timothy Tiddlefish. "I think it's becoming a bit of an – *issshooo!*"

"'Tis an issue all right," snapped Buster.
He held up the *Seafarer's News*. "See this?"
The crew looked.

The headline said:

STANDING OVATION FOR TOP ADMIRAL

Last night, in a speech to cheering crowds, Admiral Ainsley Goldglove, the celebrated pirate-catcher, said: "In my brilliant career, I've captured all the big pirate names – Blackbeard, Redbeard, Longbeard and Falsebeard Annie. I'm now about to mop up the riff-raff, starting with Buster Gutt and his tinpot crew. I'll have them in irons in no time. I stake my glove on it."

"Riff-raff!" spat Buster. "I'll get 'im for that."

"Might make more sense to just keep out of his way," said One-Eyed Ed. "Make sure there's plenty o' sea between us."

"Rubbish!" roared Buster. "No one calls me riff-raff. I'm gonna take the wind out of 'is sails, once an' for all."

"How?" asked Timothy Tiddlefish.

"Easy. I'm gonna get that perishin' gold glove off 'im an' nail it to the topmast, up by the Jolly Roger. We'll see what the papers 'ave to say about *that*."

There was a pause while the crew considered this.

"Actually," admitted Timothy Tiddlefish, "actually, it's a good idea. But how do we get it? He never takes it off. They say he sleeps in it."

Buster shrugged. "So? We'll chop 'is 'and off."

"Too messy," said Timothy, firmly. "No, we need a clever plan. And I think I might have one. Did I ever mention my Auntie Flo? She's a washerwoman…"

And Timothy told them his plan.

Chapter Two

The following day *The Bad Joke* was moored in a scruffy part of the harbour, which only rough pirates and really rude seagulls used. Timothy Tiddlefish and Threefingers Jake had gone off earlier to pay a visit to Timothy's Auntie Flo, who had proved very helpful.

Right now, they were standing in an alley leading to the smart part of the harbour, where Admiral Ainsley Goldglove's ship, *HMS Glorious*, was proudly moored.

They were both disguised as washerwomen! Timothy wore a frilly cap and matching apron over a blue dress. Jake was got up in a straw bonnet, pink skirt and brown shawl. They carried a large washing basket between them.

"Ready?" said Timothy,
sniffing.

"Just sortin' out my
bonnet," said
Threefingers
Jake.

"Hurry up!" hissed Timothy.

"I'm comin', I'm comin'. It's these flippin'
ribbons. All right, I'm ready."

Holding up their skirts, they tripped lightly over the cobbles and up the gangplank of the *HMS Glorious*.

Up on deck, Private Derek Plankton stopped dusting the deck and stared.

"Good day," fluted Timothy, bobbing a curtsey. "I'm Susan and this is my friend Alice. She's shy. Say hello to the nice sailor, Alice."

"'Ello," growled Jake, shyly scratching his stubble.

"We're the While-U-Wait Washing Service," explained Timothy. "Can we see the admiral?"

"I'll ask," said Private Derek Plankton. And he wandered off, dusting as he went.

A short time later, he was back.

"He says he'll see you," said Private Derek Plankton. "This way."

"So far, so good," whispered Timothy, as they followed him below.

Meanwhile, back at *The Bad Joke*, all remained quiet. Buster had ordered everyone to keep a low profile. Shore leave was cancelled. Talking wasn't allowed. Everyone tiptoed. Biscuits were banned, because the crunching might draw unwanted attention.

Bowzer, the ship's dog, was bored. He didn't like sitting around. He wanted to go walkies. He wanted to visit a tavern and scrounge octopus scratchings.

He wanted to chase a ball, sniff around the lobster pots, cock his leg on land for a change.

He stood on deck, sniffing at the
gangplank, which still bore the faint traces
of Timothy Tiddlefish and Threefingers
Jake, who had gone
off on a
secret walkies.
Without
him.

Why?

Where?

Had they gone to a tavern? Or to buy
him a new ball, perhaps?

Bowzer trotted down the gangplank, tail
wagging jauntily, following
his nose.

Private Derek Plankton was back dusting
the deck when Bowzer came bounding up
the gangplank of the *HMS Glorious*.

"Ooh," said Private Derek
Plankton. "Another
visitor. Hello,
doggy."

He reached out and tickled Bowzer
with his feather duster. Bowzer gave
a happy woof and rolled over.

Private Derek Plankton found a biscuit in his pocket. Bowzer ate it. Private Derek Plankton gave him another. It was love.

Chapter Three

"Well, I must say it's an excellent idea," said Admiral Ainsley Goldglove.

He was sitting in his cabin, sipping wine. Also present were Crisply Pimpleby (first officer), Seaman Scuttle (deckhand) and Monty Marshmallow (chef) who was clearing away the remains of the admiral's meal.

The admiral was in a good mood. He'd enjoyed an excellent lunch, had read a very flattering article about himself in the paper, and now two charming maidens were offering to do the entire ship's dirty laundry!

"We bring it back all nicely ironed, don't we, Alice?" trilled the maiden in blue.

"Yeah," rasped the one in pink. "And it's special rates for officers."

"Good, good," nodded the admiral. "And you'll wash anything, you say?"

"Ooh yes!" fluted the blue maiden. "Shirts, pants, socks, all the usual. And we do special items as well. Like that famous gold glove of yours, sir. That could do with a wash, couldn't it, Alice?"

"Really?" Frowning, the admiral examined his glove. "You think so?"

"Bit o' soft soap, come up a treat," growled the pink maiden.

"I don't know," pondered the admiral. "I never let it out of my sight, you see. It puts terror in the heart of any pirate when they see it flashing in the sun."

"It'd flash even more if it was clean, though, wouldn't it?" said the maiden in blue. Adding, "And you'd get it back by nightfall."

"Hmm. What do
you think, Pimpleby?"
Crisply Pimpleby
gave a smart salute.
"I say go for it, sir.
If a glove's worth
flashing, it's worth
flashing well."

"You're right," decided the admiral.
"Everything must be washed. Clothes off,
everyone! You first, Pimpleby."
"What?"

"You heard. You should set an example to the men. Your uniform is distinctly un-ship-shape," said the admiral.

"But what'll I wear? If everything's going in the wash?" panicked Pimpleby.

"How should I know? Don't bother me with details. Just do it."

Some time later, Timothy and Jake scurried up the gangplank of *The Bad Joke*, basket piled high with dirty laundry. Jake was dragging a reluctant Bowzer by the scarf. It had been really hard to coax him away from Private Derek Plankton and his delicious biscuits.

The crew hurried out on deck to meet them.
"Got it?" asked Buster, eagerly.

"Got it!" said Timothy, triumphantly
holding up the admiral's gold glove.
Everyone cheered.
"Well done, lads!"
whooped Buster.
"Right. Where's
the hammer?"

Chapter Four

Admiral Ainsley Goldglove stood anxiously on deck. Night was falling, and there was still no sign of Susan or Alice.

The admiral wore a silk dressing gown. It was rather thin and he felt quite chilly.

Mind you, he was better off than the rest of the crew, who were shivering away in a selection of ill-fitting underwear. The sort that's given to you by your granny, lies at the bottom of your drawer and is only ever used in desperation.

"Where *are* they?"
fretted the admiral.
"Where are our *clothes*?
And more importantly,
where's my glove?"

"Sir! Look!" gasped

Crisply Pimpleby, suddenly. He pointed

out to sea, his face a mask of horror.

Sailing towards them was *The Bad Joke*, with the Jolly Roger flapping. And pegged to the rigging and pinned all over the sails was…

"Our laundry!" moaned Crisply Pimpleby.
"Gutt's got it!"

He had too. There it was, displayed on high for all to see. And for the final insult, nailed boldly to the topmast was…

"My glove!" shrieked the admiral. "Look what he's done to *my gold glove*!"

Over on board *The Bad Joke*, Buster and
the boys were really enjoying themselves.

"Riff-raff, eh?" bellowed Buster, as they
drew abreast. "That'll learn yer!"

"We got yer gold glove, we got yer gold
glove!" chanted Jimmy Maggot, Crasher
Jackson and One-Eyed Ed. Timothy
Tiddlefish made rude faces and
Threefingers Jake hurled his bonnet in
the air.

Only Bowzer didn't join in. He had
something else on his mind. He had spotted
his new friend, Private Derek Plankton.
And that meant… *Biscuits!*

Before anyone could stop him, Bowzer
leaped over the rail ...

... hurtled down into the sea and began to doggy-paddle.

"Oi!" shouted Buster. "Bowzer! What you playin' at? Come back, you traitor!"

Admiral Ainsley Goldglove saw his chance. "That's it!" he urged. "Here, boy! Keep going, there's a good dog!"

Bowzer was a good swimmer.
In no time at all, he was
on board the enemy
ship, all wet and
happy and
covering
Private Derek
Plankton with slobber.

"Oh – *sharksbum*!" groaned Buster.
"That's torn it."

"You see?" crowed Admiral Ainsley
Goldglove. "Foiled again, Gutt!"

He was right. It was stalemate. Buster had the glove, but the admiral had Bowzer.

So what did they do? They did a swap, of course.

At midnight, watched by both crews, Timothy Tiddlefish and Private Derek Plankton rowed ashore and met on the jetty.

Timothy gave Private Derek Plankton all
the grubby laundry back, plus the gold glove.

Private Derek Plankton solemnly handed
over the reluctant Bowzer.

They then got back into their rowing
boats and made for their separate ships.

Buster and the crew were very relieved to get Bowzer back. But Bowzer wasn't so pleased. He was very put out at being parted yet again from Private Derek Plankton and his delicious biscuits.

He went all sad and sulky until Buster opened a new sack of octopus scratchings. He cheered up then all right.

"Nice to 'ave 'im back 'ome," remarked
Buster to Timothy Tiddlefish, as they
watched Bowzer getting stuck in. He gave a
sigh. "Shame we didn't get to keep the gold
glove, though."

"Shame we came out of it looking so silly
too," said Timothy, gloomily. "All that
effort for nothing. Let's hope the papers
don't find out."

Sadly, though – they did.

ADMIRAL MAKES DOG'S DINNER OF CAPTURE

It was red faces all round when Admiral Ainsley Goldglove came face to face with Buster Gutt and his gormless crew!